RON THE ROYAL GUARD

To Lancashire Digital Superstars
and Eric Martindale
~ D Y

For Michelle and David
~ P B

First published in the UK in 2019
This edition published 2019
by New Frontier Publishing Europe Ltd.
Uncommon, 126 New King's Rd, Fulham, London SW6 4LZ
www.newfrontierpublishing.co.uk

ISBN: 978-1-912858-40-8
Text copyright © 2019 Dean Yipadee
Illustrations copyright © 2019 Paul Beavis
The rights of Dean Yipadee to be identified as the author and
Paul Beavis to be identified as the illustrator of this work have been asserted.

A CIP catalogue record for this book
is available from the British Library.

Designed by Verity Clark

Printed in China
10 9 8 7 6 5 4 3 2

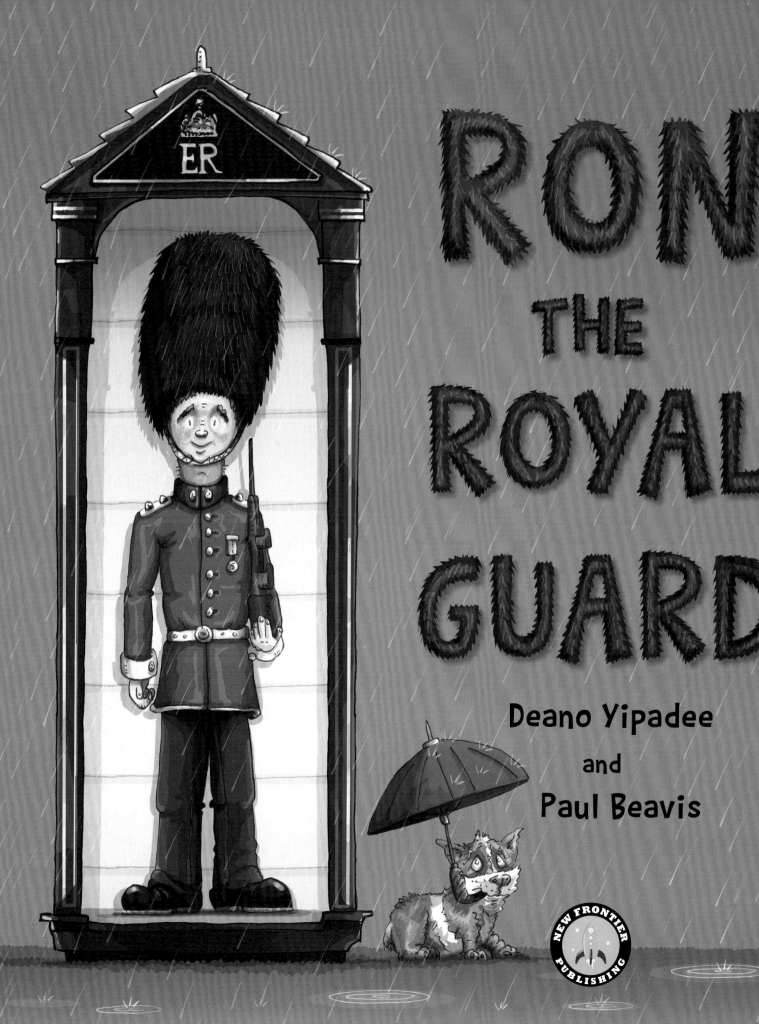

RON THE ROYAL GUARD

Deano Yipadee
and
Paul Beavis

Ron is the Royal Guard
At the palace every day,

Looking after royals
While the corgis run and play.

Before he starts his shift,
He enjoys a **cup of tea**,

And on some
British **sunny** days

He can **guzzle**
almost **three!**

'I am **Ron**, the Royal Guard,
Here by **Royal** Decree!

Standing very,
very **still,**

*** **star** *** of
the odd **selfie!'**

One day something felt wrong,
And with some **urgency**

Ron cried,

'someone
help me,
please!

He **marched**
from side
to side

And as the funny feeling **grew,**
Ron **hollered** to the Queen:

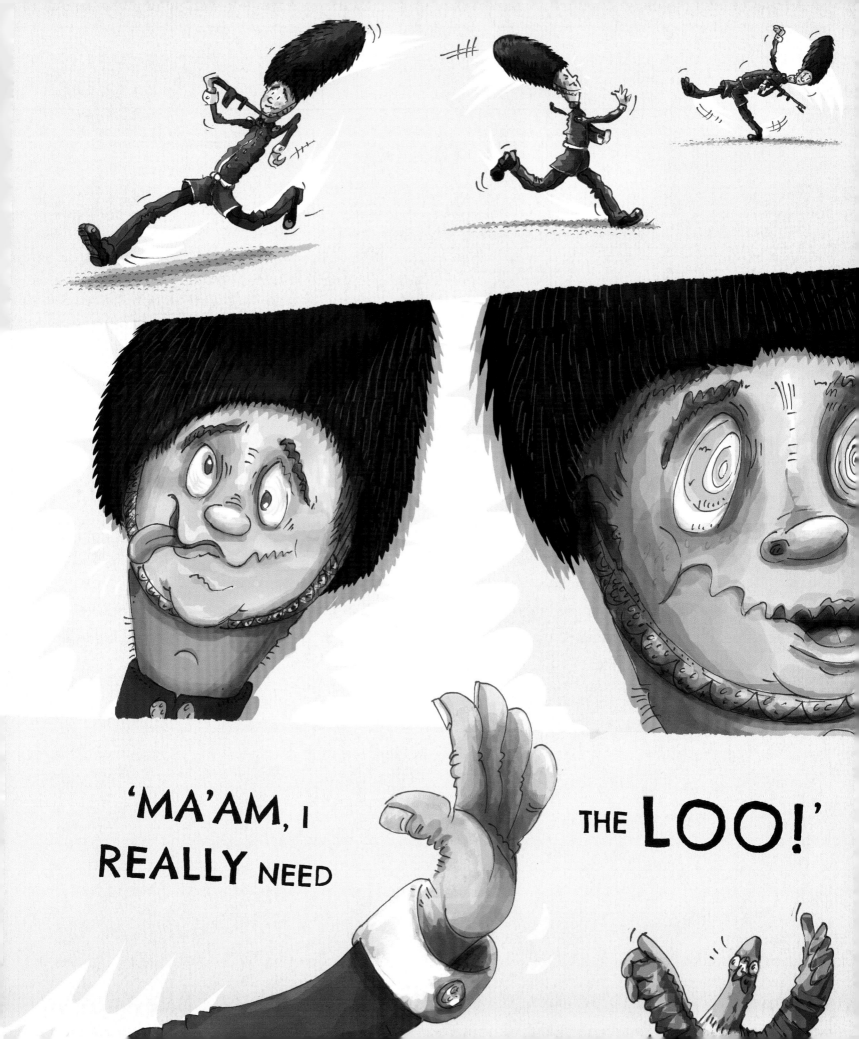

'I am **Ron**, the Royal Guard,
Here by **Royal Decree!**

Ron **criss-crossed**
his legs

And **bobbled** **UP** and *down.*

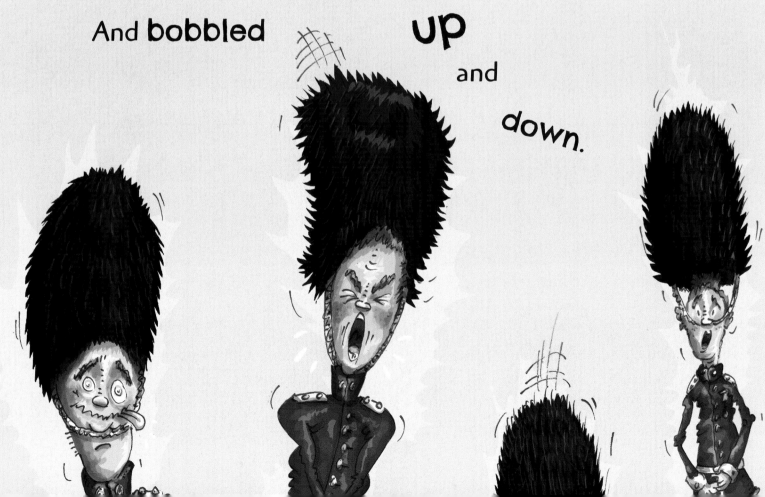

Then he had a
great idea

As he **jiggled**
round and round . . .

If there was someone else
Who'd put on his outfit

Then he could **sneak** to the **lavatory**
For just a little bit!

'I am **Ron**,
the **Royal Guard**,

Here by
Royal Decree!

Does **anyone** have a **dad** with them

Who could **dress up** as **ME**?'

But there was **no-one** to be seen,
Just the Queen's little **dog** . . .

So Ron thought **fast** …

and changed his **plan**
To get him to the **bog**.

One **corgi** wore his **coat**.

Another wore his **hat**.

The rest **stacked up** inside his **trousers** –
And that took care of that!

It was almost **perfect**!
No-one had a clue . . .

Except that **chap** in underpants
Who was **dashing** to the **loo!**

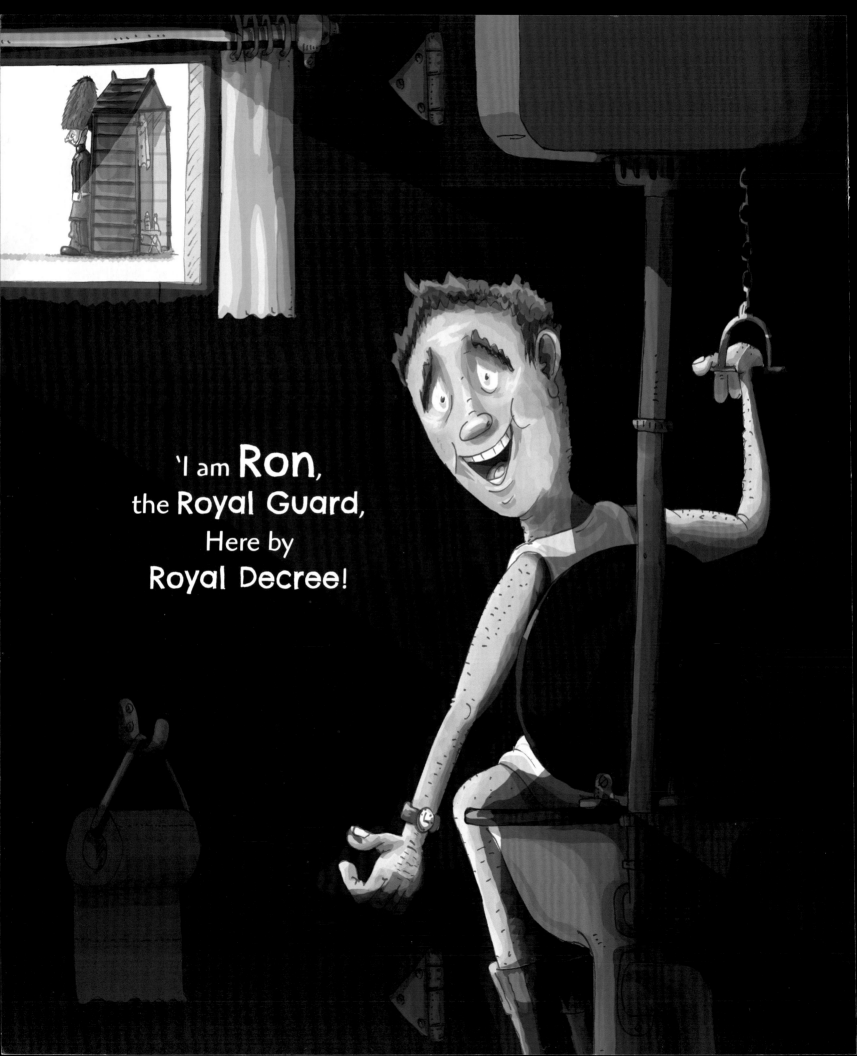

'I am Ron,
the Royal Guard,
Here by
Royal Decree!

And if I seem **barking** mad,
I might be **busting**
for a . . .'